WONDERFUL WORLD OF
EARTH

As a 2008 Milken Educator, I take the challenge of reviewing educational materials seriously. As I examined the Disney Learning series, I was impressed by the vivid graphics, captivating content, and introductory humor provided by the various Disney characters. But I decided I should take the material to the true experts, my third grade students, and listen to what they had to say. In their words, "The series is interesting. The books are really fun and eye-catching! They make me want to learn more. I can't wait until the books are in the bookstore!" They looked forward to receiving a new book from the series with as much anticipation as a birthday present or a holiday gift. Based on their expert opinion, this series will be a part of my classroom library. I may even purchase two sets to meet their demand.

Barbara Black
2008 Milken Educator
National Board Certified Teacher—Middle Childhood Generalist
Certified 2001/Renewed 2010

For information address Disney Press,
114 Fifth Avenue, New York, New York 10011-5690.

Visit www.disneybooks.com
Printed in China
ISBN 978-1-4231-4939-2
T425-2382-5-12153
First Edition
Written by Thea Feldman
Fact-checked by Barbara Berliner
All rights reserved.

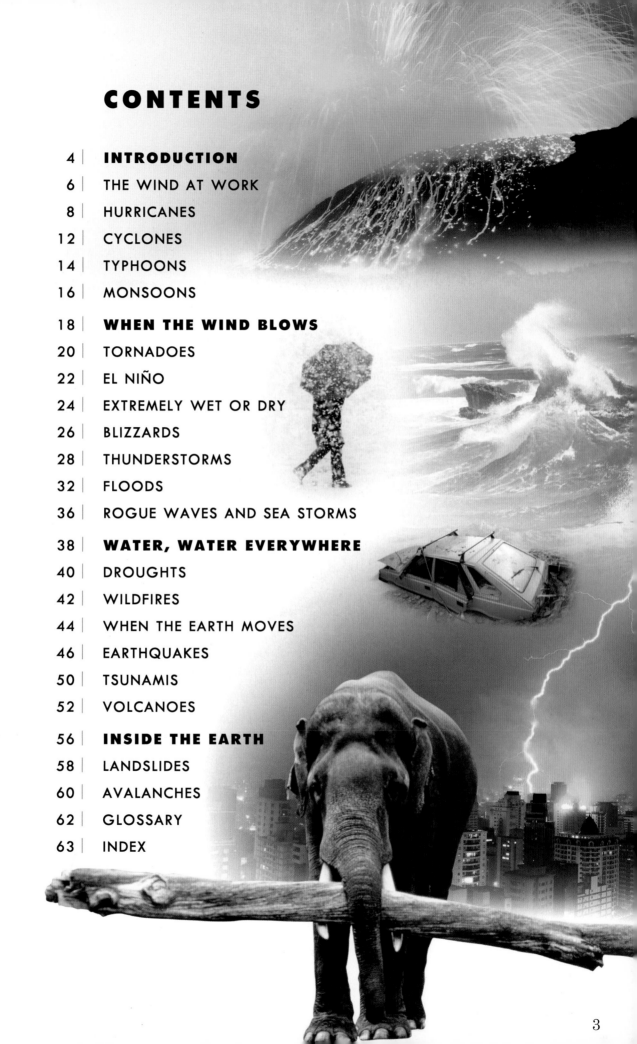

CONTENTS

WONDERFUL WORLD OF
EARTH

OUR PLANET IS ALWAYS IN MOTION

You don't feel the Earth spinning and circling around the Sun. But you do experience the planet's other forces at work: the wind blowing, the rain falling, or the ground shaking.

EARTHLY EXTREMES

The wind can come as a gentle breeze or a fierce hurricane. Water falls in a refreshing drizzle or a deadly thunderstorm. The ground's shaking can be caused by an earthquake, volcanic eruption, or landslide. Mild or extreme, these events are all part of the natural workings of the Earth.

EARLY EXPLANATIONS

Extreme events and natural disasters have always affected life on Earth. This frightened ancient people. To cope, they invented folklore to explain the Earth's displays of power. They believed that gods in the heavens were creating floods, droughts, monsoons, and more.

THE SCIENCE BEHIND IT

Scientific explanations have replaced myths and legends. Scientists now know that wind, water, or motion may be the driving force behind an extreme event. One alone can also cause others. Strong windstorms often bring lots of rain, which can cause floods and mud slides. A lack of wind in one place can cause droughts in some places and floods in others.

There is concern that our planet is getting warmer. Climatologists (scientists who study the weather conditions) believe extreme events and natural disasters may happen more often because of this.

PEOPLE AND PLACES

An extreme event is about more than just the awesome power of nature and the science behind it. It is also about the people and places affected. A blizzard, wildfire, or El Niño can mean death and destruction to a community or country. Earth's natural forces have always awed us with their power and ability to alter lives and landscapes. Let's explore some of the most extreme events on Earth.

ARCTIC

PACIFIC

NORTH
AMERICA

ATLANTIC

SOUTH
AMERICA

THE WIND AT WORK

Hurricanes, monsoons, tornadoes, and El Niños
are all powerful examples of extreme weather.
The thing they have in common? Wind.
Whether the wind is roaring at high speeds,
changing direction, or just not blowing its
usual way, it is the driving force behind some
of nature's most monstrous natural disasters.

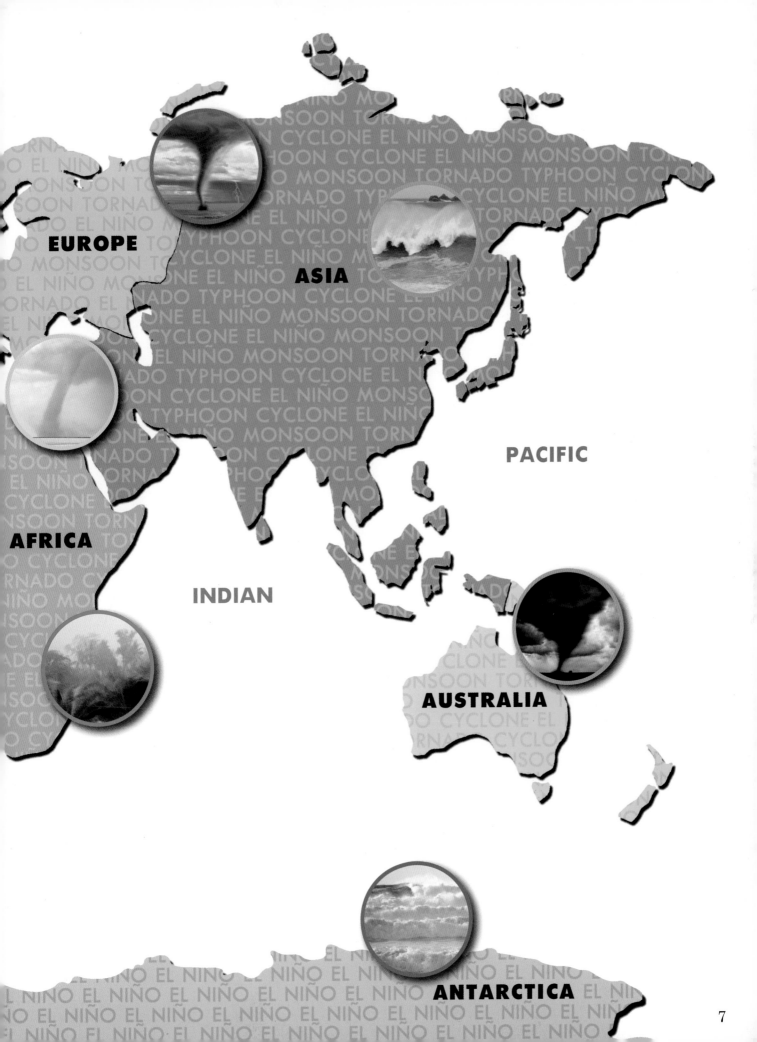

EUROPE

ASIA

PACIFIC

AFRICA

INDIAN

AUSTRALIA

ANTARCTICA

HURRICANES

A hurricane's strong winds and pelting rain can destroy buildings, cars, and bridges, costing billions of dollars in damage.

Hold on tight!

Most hurricanes move at speeds between 15–20 miles per hour. They usually don't last more than 24 hours once they reach land.

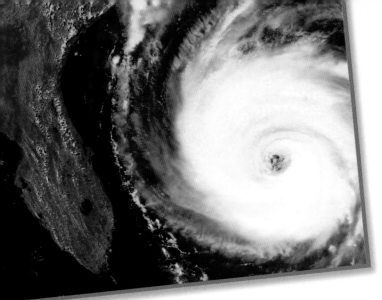

Hurricane Fran off the coast of Florida

WHERE DO HURRICANES HIT?

Hurricanes form over the **Atlantic Ocean**. They may hit Central, North, and South America, the Caribbean Islands, and Bermuda. In the United States, hurricanes strike states along the **east coast** of the Atlantic Ocean and the Gulf of Mexico. **Florida** is hit most often.

Category 4 hurricane

HOW DO HURRICANES HAPPEN?

A **hurricane** forms on the open ocean when three things come together in the right mix: **temperature**, **moisture**, and **wind**. When the ocean's surface is warm enough, the sea water evaporates. This moisture returns to the air. Wind near the ocean's surface combines with this warm air and moisture to create a storm. The storm makes the air even hotter! Then the **hot air** and the winds rise. If these conditions continue, the storm becomes a hurricane.

HOW STRONG ARE WINDS IN A HURRICANE?

The weakest hurricane has winds that blow **74 miles per hour**. Two American scientists developed the **Hurricane Wind Scale** to categorize a hurricane's intensity.

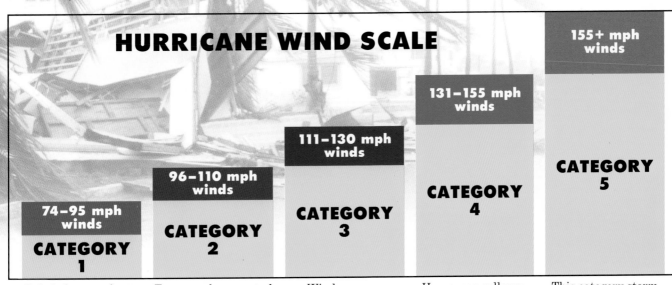

HURRICANE WIND SCALE

74–95 mph winds **CATEGORY 1**	**96–110 mph winds** **CATEGORY 2**	**111–130 mph winds** **CATEGORY 3**	**131–155 mph winds** **CATEGORY 4**	**155+ mph winds** **CATEGORY 5**
Debris from roofs can fly around, windows can break, and chimneys can topple.	Trees can be uprooted, and power outages can occur when overhead power lines come down.	Windows may be blown out. Uprooted trees can block roadways.	Homes can collapse. Damage to water supplies may occur, causing shortages.	This category storm has the strength to bring down office and apartment buildings.

HURRICANES

In 1953, the National Hurricane Center in the United States began to use human names for hurricanes. A name is retired if a storm is particularly violent, deadly, or costly. Retired hurricane names include Mitch and Katrina.

The outer part of a hurricane is called the "rain band." The next layer, where the wind is strongest, is called the "eye wall." The center, called "the eye," is where winds are relatively light, with little or no rain.

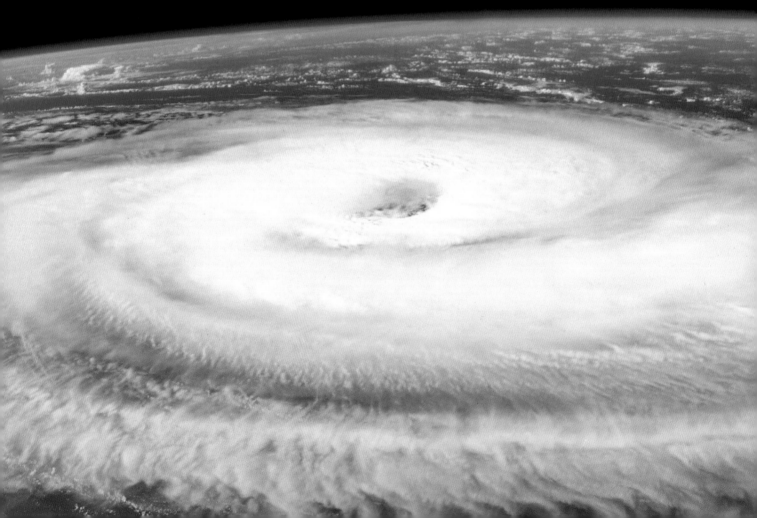

HOW ARE HURRICANES NAMED?

The World **Meteorological** Organization is in charge of naming. There are **six lists** beginning with an "A" name. These six lists are **rotated** and then **reused**. So, for example, the list beginning with Arlene used in 2011 will be used again in 2017.

Flooded streets after Hurricane Katrina

The aftermath of Hurricane Katrina

WHO GOT THE WORST OF HURRICANE KATRINA?

Hurricane Katrina struck the United States in **August 2005** as a **Category 3** hurricane. The storm's wind and water ravaged the **coastal areas** of Louisiana, Mississippi, and Alabama. New Orleans, Louisiana, was hit particularly hard. Ocean **waves** and rising river waters overtopped the **levees** designed to protect the city. Much of New Orleans was underwater. More than 1,000 people died in Louisiana and another 200 in Mississippi.

HOW ARE HURRICANES MONITORED?

In the U.S., the National Hurricane Center uses equipment such as **satellites** to monitor hurricanes as they develop in the ocean. When a storm begins to form, the NHC often calls in the **Hurricane Hunters**, a special squadron of the U.S. Air Force Reserve. They fly right into a Category 3 or higher storm to measure the **wind force**, temperature, humidity, and air pressure. The information helps the NHC determine where a storm is going to strike land.

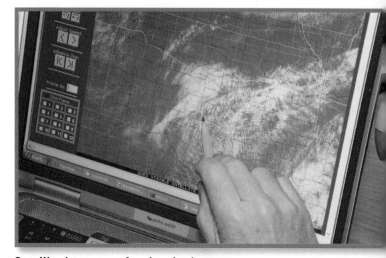

Satellite imagery of a developing storm

CYCLONES

Cyclones sure can fly!

A cyclone can hit land with the same strong winds and torrential downpours as a hurricane. But a cyclone forms in a different part of the world—over the Indian Ocean.

A cyclone rotates clockwise as it moves over the ocean and on the land. A hurricane rotates the opposite way—counterclockwise.

HOW STRONG
ARE WINDS IN A CYCLONE?

A **Category 5** cyclone has wind gusts in excess of 173 miles per hour. **Cyclone Olivia** exceeded that. In 1996, this cyclone hit northwest Australia with wind gusts of **253.5 miles per hour**! It destroyed a number of houses and caused several injuries. Miraculously, nobody died.

Cyclone Billy off the western coast of Australia

WHAT PLACES GET A LOT OF CYCLONES?

An average of 13 **cyclones** a year form over the ocean waters near **Australia**. Only about three or four become severe. Wind speeds can reach **73 to 124 miles per hour**. The Republic of Madagascar lies off the east coast of southern Africa. It is in the path of cyclones that cross the western Indian Ocean. Every year, it is **battered** by several, resulting in **winds** and rains that wash out roads, isolate villages, and affect hundreds of thousands of people.

A flooded road in Madagascar

A large ocean swell caused by a cyclone

DO CYCLONES BRING
LOTS OF RAIN?

Rainfall during a cyclone can be **intense**. In 1966, Cyclone Denise dumped **3.7 feet** of rain in 12 hours on La Reunion Island, east of **Madagascar**.

TYPHOONS

What kind of storm generates hurricane-like winds and cyclone-like rain but forms over the western Pacific Ocean and moves into the China Sea? A typhoon!

That's a lean, mean, blowing machine!

Typhoons strike the coasts of Southeast Asia, the Philippines, China, Taiwan, and Japan. Typhoons are most common from July through November.

WHAT COUNTRY GETS HIT BY THE MOST TYPHOONS?

The **Philippines**, a nation of 7,100 islands, sits right in the path of typhoons that form over the **Pacific Ocean**. On average, **20 typhoons** strike the Philippines every year!

Typhoon approaching a beach in the Philippines

The aftermath of Typhoon Nina in the Philippines

CAN ANYTHING STOP A TYPHOON?

No! Typhoons (or hurricanes or cyclones) can't be stopped. But mountains can help tame the **raging** winds. **Taiwan**, located 75 miles off the coast of Asia, sits at the edge of the Pacific Ocean. It is a prime target for typhoons. But the island's 12,000-foot-high **mountains** work as natural shields against the whipping winds.

WHAT WAS ONE OF THE WORST TYPHOONS EVER?

Typhoon Tip slammed into southern Japan in 1979 with wind speeds of **190 miles per hour**. Tip was huge—at its largest it was 1,350 miles across. Tip caused **massive flooding**, shipwrecks, and millions of dollars in damages to property and crops. Ninety-nine people died as a result of this super typhoon.

Typhoon in Japan

MONSOONS

Wind is a basic ingredient of monsoons, as well as hurricanes, cyclones, and typhoons. But a monsoon is a different kind of storm, with a unique way of forming.

There's nothing tiny about a monsoon!

Wet monsoons happen in the heat of the summer and on every continent except Antarctica.

Floodwaters after a heavy monsoon in India

IS THERE ANYTHING GOOD ABOUT A MONSOON?

In southwestern **India**, monsoons bring rain and relief from temperatures that can top 100°F by June. The rains **help plants** grow—including farmers' crops, **grass** for elephants, and **fruit** for monkeys. Without the monsoon rains, southwestern India becomes so dry that people can die from famine and other heat-related problems.

WHAT CAUSES A MONSOON?

Scientists think a few things happen together to cause a **monsoon**. First, the sun heats the air over a plateau—an area of level high ground. Second, while the temperature on land rises, the air temperature over **the ocean** cools. The hot air over the plateau rises. The cooler ocean air fills the space left. This shifting of air or change in **wind** direction creates a monsoon.

Damage to houses after a monsoon in India

ARE MONSOONS DANGEROUS?

A **monsoon** causes too much rain in a short amount of time. This can cause a **flood**. Plants and homes get washed away, and people are **displaced** or even killed. A monsoon can bring life, but it can also bring **danger**. Some parts of India receive up to 40 feet of rain in less than 4 months. The town of Cherrapunji in India once got over 3 feet of rain in just one day!

Heavy monsoon rain in Burma

WHEN THE WIND BLOWS

Wind is everywhere. You can't see it or touch it. But it is one of the most powerful forces of nature. So what exactly *is* it?

SEA BREEZES AND LAND BREEZES

Along beaches, coastlines, and large lakes, strong **breezes** commonly blow in the afternoon. Air over the land is **warmed** by the sun all day; that air is ready to rise in the afternoon. **Cooler** air from over the sea moves in. This is known as a sea breeze. After the sun goes down, the land cools more quickly than the sea, so the reverse happens. This is called a land breeze.

MOVING AIR

Wind is the **movement** of the air around you. Because the sun warms the Earth unevenly, air temperatures vary. During the day, the air over water tends to be **cooler**. Air over land tends to be **hotter**. Hot air rises. Cool air stays closer to the ground.

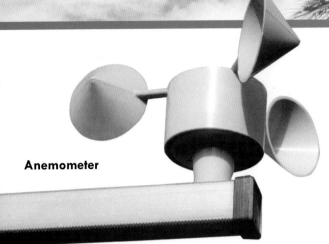

Anemometer

MEASURING WIND
SPEED
AND FORCE

An **anemometer** measures wind speed. A simple anemometer has several **cups** mounted on it. Wind blows into the cups and makes them **turn**. The anemometer gauges how quickly the cups turn. This is the same as the speed of the wind.

The **Beaufort Scale** measures the force of wind over land or water. The scale ranks wind from a calm **force 0** (about 1 mile per hour) up to a hurricane-strength **force 12**.

HARNESSING
THE WIND

In 1887, the first wind **turbine** capable of generating electricity was developed. Today, wind farms all over the world harness the wind for **energy**. Wind power could become an important energy source. Wind is not only a "clean" energy (it doesn't pollute the air), it is also a **renewable** source. We will never run out of wind.

WORKING
WITH THE WIND

People have been using the **force** of wind to power machines and get their work done for centuries. The use of wind power dates back to 5th-century **Persia** (Iran today). There the first **windmills** were created to water crops. The invention reached Europe in the 12th century, where it was also used for turning **grindstones** in flour mills.

WINDIEST
PLACE ON EARTH

Commonwealth Bay in Antarctica often records winds racing at about **200 miles per hour**! This is faster than the strongest hurricanes, cyclones, or typhoons. It even ranks up there with the **most powerful** tornadoes!

Wind turbines in Spain

TORNADOES

Look at that tornado go!

If you ever see a huge, spinning cloud heading toward you, you'd better hope it's far away! You don't want to be anywhere near one of these fast-moving storms. They can have the most powerful, violent winds of all.

A tornado is a tightly turning funnel-shaped cloud. That huge, twisting mass has to touch the ground to reach official tornado status.

WHERE DO **MOST TORNADOES** STRIKE?

Tornadoes strike most often in an area of approximately **10 states** in the midwestern U.S. This area east of the Rocky Mountains is nicknamed **Tornado Alley**.

Tornadoes can happen any time of year or any time of day. In Tornado Alley, most occur from March through May.

HOW MUCH **DAMAGE** CAN A TORNADO **CAUSE?**

Meteorologists use technology called **Doppler** radar to track **tornadoes**.

Once a tornado has passed, its strength is determined by how much destruction it left behind. The storm is given a rating based on the **Enhanced Fujita** (EF) Scale that works like this:

WHERE ELSE CAN **TORNADOES** HAPPEN?

In Europe, the **United Kingdom** usually sees the most tornadoes. In South America it is **Argentina**. South Africa gets the most tornadoes in Africa. In Asia, **twisters** happen in China, Japan, the Philippines, India, and Bangladesh. Very few tornadoes strike Australia. In North America, Canada gets about 100 of them per year. But the winner is the **U.S.** with about **1,000** tornadoes each year—more than the rest of the world combined.

Tornado damage in Franklin, Kansas, U.S.

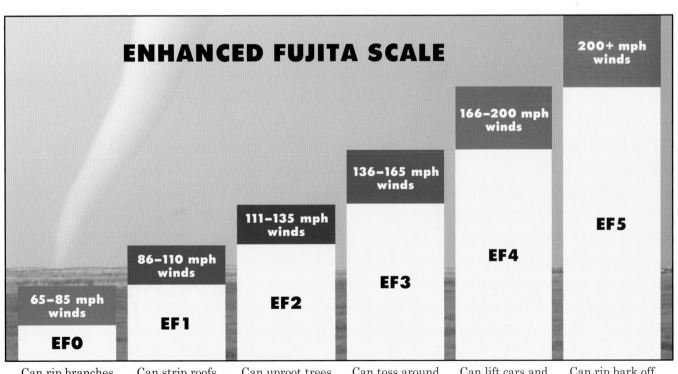

ENHANCED FUJITA SCALE

EF0	EF1	EF2	EF3	EF4	EF5
65–85 mph winds	86–110 mph winds	111–135 mph winds	136–165 mph winds	166–200 mph winds	200+ mph winds
Can rip branches off trees and toss debris around	Can strip roofs from houses and overturn mobile homes	Can uproot trees	Can toss around jagged pieces of steel, glass, and wood	Can lift cars and crush houses	Can rip bark off trees and lift houses off their foundations

EL NIÑO

An El Niño begins when there is an unusual warming of sea surface temperatures in the central Pacific Ocean, and along the equator and the coasts of Peru and Ecuador in South America.

El Niños sure can pack a punch!

On average, an El Niño happens once every four years. The effect lasts about 18 months.

WHY ARE PERU AND ECUADOR AFFECTED?

The imaginary line of the **equator** cuts through the northern part of **Ecuador**. Much of that country's coastline is located just below the equator. **Peru** is Ecuador's neighbor directly to the south, so all of its coastline is close to the equator, too.

Flooding in Peru

Map showing Ecuador (red) and Peru (green)

WHAT'S THE **WORST** THING ABOUT AN EL NIÑO?

Usually the coasts of Ecuador and Peru experience something called an **upwelling**. The deeper, colder ocean water moves up toward the surface. This colder water contains **nutrients** important to fish nearer the surface. When an **El Niño** happens, the upwelling doesn't. The fish population dwindles or even dies off. People in the fishing industry also suffer.

CAN ANY **GOOD** COME FROM AN **EL NIÑO?**

If an **El Niño** event can be predicted, people can prepare. With enough notice, fishermen could arrange to **harvest** shrimp and other food sources that do well in warmer water. Farmers can **plant** rice and beans in places that are normally too dry to support these crops.

Indonesian rice farmer

BLIZZARDS

Brrrr!

Snow. Who doesn't like to walk in it, build a snowman, or sled down a hill? But when too much snow falls, things can turn chilling—and deadly.

Blizzards can occur wherever temperatures reach freezing—32°F.

WHAT IS A BLIZZARD?

A **blizzard** is a snowstorm with winds over **35 miles per hour**. Snow falls so heavily or is driven so hard by the **wind** that you can only see one quarter of a mile or less. When these conditions last for at least three hours, you're officially in a blizzard—the most severe kind of **snowstorm**!

A blizzard in New York City

Snowy road in a blizzard

WHAT WERE SOME OF THE WORST BLIZZARDS?

The **Iran Blizzard** of **1972** dumped more than **10 feet** of snow across that country in seven days. Some parts of southern Iran received 26 feet of snow, and 4,000 people died.

The **Great Blizzard** of **1888** slammed into the East Coast of the United States, shutting down **New York City** and the surrounding area. Elevated trains were stuck, horse-drawn cars couldn't move, and all the telegraph and telephone wires went down. Snowdrifts as high as **30 feet** kept New York City at a standstill for about a week.

WHY ARE BLIZZARDS SO DANGEROUS?

Extreme cold is the number one danger during a blizzard. It can cause **frostbite** when you lose feeling in your fingers, toes, nose, or any exposed area. People can lose fingers and toes from frostbite!

If your body temperature drops just four degrees after being out in the cold, you can slip into **hypothermia**. Hypothermia is a dangerous—and sometimes deadly—condition in which your body starts to shut down.

THUNDERSTORMS

Flash! Boom! A thunderstorm, complete with streaks of lightning in the sky and rumbling thunder, is a spectacular display of Mother Nature at work.

Mother Nature sure seems angry!

Around the world, lightning hits the ground about 100 times a second—that's 8 million times a day!

Thunderstorm with lightning

WHAT IS LIGHTNING?

Lightning starts as electrical **energy** inside some clouds. When that energy is **discharged**, it creates lightning. There are three types of lightning **strikes**. The most common takes place inside a single cloud. The second kind takes place between two clouds. The third kind, cloud-to-ground lightning, is the one that is most **dangerous**.

Lightning bolt hitting a sign

HOW FAST IS LIGHTNING?
HOW HOT CAN LIGHTNING GET?

A single **flash** of lightning travels at **60,000 miles per second**! That's where the expression "moving at lightning speed" comes from.

A lightning bolt can heat the air from 18,000°F to 54,000°F! At its coolest, a lightning bolt is almost twice as hot as the surface of the **Sun**! Lightning is the most powerful—and hottest—electrical force on Earth.

Lightning over a city

WHAT HAPPENS IF YOU GET STRUCK BY LIGHTNING?

About **2,000 people** are struck by lightning every year. Around 70% of those have severe **injuries**, ranging from burns to brain damage. Lightning kills about 20% of the people it hits! The **electric charge** passes through the body and disappears into the ground. Sometimes the lightning will exit through a hole it burns in a person's shoe!

THUNDERSTORMS

When lightning heats the air so much and so quickly, the air expands and creates a sound wave we hear as thunder.

Eeek! Save me!

Thunder can commonly be heard up to 15 miles away from where the lightning discharges. When it's farther away, it may sound more like a rumble than like a crack.

WHAT CAN KEEP A
BUILDING SAFE
FROM LIGHTNING?

A **lightning rod** keeps the building and everyone inside safe. A lightning rod is a metal spike fixed to the **highest** point on a building. A metal strip runs from the rod down the entire length of the building and into the **ground**. That way, if lightning does strike the rod, it will travel down the strip and go directly into the ground.

Lightning hitting a lightning rod

CAN LIGHTNING
HURT YOU
IF YOU'RE INSIDE?

Sometimes **lightning** doesn't hit a lightning rod. Instead it can hit anything made of **metal**, such as wires or pipes, and travel through whatever it hits. During a thunderstorm, it's best to avoid contact with any **electrical** equipment. It's also not a good time to take a bath or shower because of the metal plumbing pipes. Talking on a landline phone indoors during a thunderstorm is actually the number one cause of lightning **injuries** in the United States!

Lightning hitting buildings in Taichung City, Taiwan

CAN LIGHTNING
STRIKE TWICE
IN THE SAME PLACE?

Yes, it can! The **Eiffel Tower** in Paris, France, and the Empire State Building in New York in the United States each get hit over **20 times** a year! **Tall buildings** in other cities have also been struck more than once, including the Petronas Towers in Kuala Lumpur, Malaysia, and the CN Tower in Toronto, Canada.

Lightning bolt hitting the Eiffel Tower

FLOODS

A flood can happen when the waters of a river or other body of water rise slowly until they overflow the banks. A flash flood can happen in hours.

Don't leave me!

Okay.

A flash flood is usually more dangerous than a slow-rising flood.

WHAT IS AN EXAMPLE OF A SLOW RISING FLOOD?

The **Amazon** River flows for nearly 4,000 miles through South America. Every year, the area has a rainy season. About **6.5 feet** of rain falls. The Amazon can slowly rise more than 30 feet. Then it overflows, creating the world's **largest** flooded forest. Nutrients from the water actually nourish the soil in the forest!

The Amazon River

DO FLASH FLOODS REALLY HAPPEN "IN A FLASH"?

Sort of. A **flash flood** usually happens within 6 hours of a severe rainstorm. Sometimes, a hurricane-force storm can cause waves more than **10 feet high**! These waves come crashing over barriers in what is called a **storm surge**. In **1953**, the North Sea flooded. This set off deadly storm surges across parts of the Netherlands, the United Kingdom, and Belgium. Nearly 2,000 people were killed. **Hurricane Katrina** swept across the Gulf of Mexico in 2005. It made landfall directly over New Orleans, Louisiana. More than 1,500 people died and hundreds of thousands were left homeless.

CAN A FLOOD BE A GOOD THING?

Yes! In **ancient Egypt**, people living along the Nile River relied on it as a source of drinking water and for transportation. They also grew their crops along the river's banks. The Nile would overflow every year and deposit **nutrient-rich** soil that was very good for these crops.

A boat on the Nile River

Submerged cars in floodwater

ROGUE WAVES AND SEA STORMS

For centuries, seamen have told stories of giant waves that threaten to swallow up their ships. Most people thought these stories of "rogue" waves were tall tales. But scientists now believe that rogue waves actually do happen.

Surf's way up!

A rogue wave is an extremely tall wave that rises up within a set of smaller waves.

CAN A SEA STORM
SINK A SHIP?

Oh, yes! A ship is no match for an angry sea or **rogue wave**. The **European Space Agency** (ESA) uses satellites to monitor ocean conditions, sea storms, and rogue waves. The agency reports that in 20 years, more than 200 **supertankers** and container ships sank. That means an average of 10 ships a year were overwhelmed by the **force** of ocean water pounding into them.

Supertanker at sea off the coast of Alaska

ARE ROGUE WAVES
UNUSUAL?

Scientists once thought a rogue wave could happen only **once every 10,000 years**. But ESA studies show that rogue waves can—and do—happen much more frequently. In **2001**, during a three-week period, the ESA's MaxWave project detected 10 huge rogue waves. Each was more than **80 feet tall**!

WHERE DO THE MOST ROGUE WAVES HAPPEN?

Cape Agulhas, at the southern tip of **Africa**, has more rogue waves than any other place. The waters of the Indian and Atlantic oceans meet here. Walls of water **95 feet tall** have been reported.

Not all rogue waves happen in ocean waters. Some have been reported in lakes. In 1975, the S.S. *Edmund Fitzgerald*, a freighter, sank while traveling on **Lake Superior** between Canada and the United States. The cause was thought to be a rogue wave.

Cape Agulhas

WATER, WATER EVERYWHERE

About 71% of Earth is covered by water. Most of this is ocean water. About 2% of the planet's water lies in freshwater lakes, rivers, ponds, and streams. What about all the water that falls from the sky? How did it get up there in the first place? And what makes it fall?

PUTTING WATER TO WORK

Falling water can move wheels and create the **energy** needed to power mills and other machinery.

Using water power to **generate electricity** began in the late 19th century. Using water to generate electricity (hydroelectricity) is growing every year. Today, it accounts for about 20% of worldwide electricity production. **Hydroelectricity** is considered an environmentally friendly, renewable source of energy.

Hydroelectric dam

THE WATER CYCLE

Just as the Sun heats the air, it also heats Earth's bodies of water. The water eventually gets hot enough to **evaporate**. It turns into water vapor that **rises** into the air. When it cools, the vapor turns back into a liquid that comes together to form **clouds**. Water builds up inside the clouds. When conditions are right, the clouds release the water. This **precipitation** falls back to Earth and its bodies of water. The cycle keeps repeating itself.

WATER'S DISGUISES

Water falls from the clouds as **rain**, freezing rain, ice pellets, hailstones, or **snow**. Inside tall, anvil-shaped clouds called **cumulonimbus** clouds, hailstones begin to form as freezing **drops** of rain. The wind pushes the drops up and down inside the cloud. Then the drops get coated in layers of ice until they get bigger and bigger and become hailstones that fall to the ground.

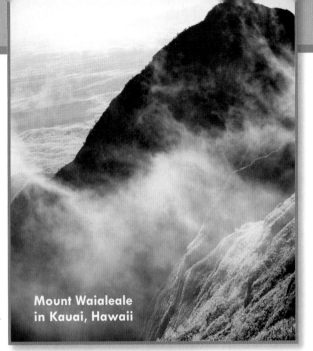

Mount Waialeale in Kauai, Hawaii

WETTEST
PLACE ON EARTH

On average, more than **451** inches of rain fall each year on **Mt. Waialeale**, Hawaii, in the U.S. That's more than 37 inches every month. Many places don't get that much in an entire year!

FROM
DROPLET
TO RAINDROP

A hailstone grows by putting on layers of freezing rain. A rain **droplet** grows by bumping into other droplets. A droplet becomes a raindrop once it measures **.02 inches across**. If a raindrop reaches .15 inches, it will usually split in two.

HAILSTONES HURT

Because they are solid **ice**, hailstones can be very hard—and they can hurt! Most hailstones are only about the size of a pea.

In **2010**, hail fell during a thunderstorm in **South Dakota** in the U.S. A single hailstone was found that was **8 inches** in diameter. It weighed almost **2 pounds**! Imagine being hit by that!

DROUGHTS

If an area doesn't have enough water, that can lead to a drought. Unlike other extreme weather conditions, a drought happens slowly—but it is still a dangerous and deadly situation.

Water is essential for crops to grow and for people and animals to drink. Without enough water to grow crops and nourish livestock, people can starve.

WHAT CAUSES A DROUGHT?

It can be caused by a **lack** of rainfall or snowfall. It can also happen when the water supply in an area isn't enough to meet everyone's needs. A drought can also occur when there isn't enough **moisture** in the soil for crops to grow.

Atacama Desert

Man on dry lakebed, Lake Powell, Utah

WHERE IS THE DRIEST PLACE ON EARTH?

It's the **Atacama Desert**, located in the Andes Mountains of **Chile** in South America. Some parts of it only get about **.004 inches** of rain per year. Other parts haven't gotten any rain for hundreds of years! But the desert is not suffering from a drought. That amount of rain is considered normal for the area.

WHAT ARE SOME OF THE WORST DROUGHTS FROM HISTORY?

In the **United States**, one drought lasted for **eight years** and affected 50 million acres of crops and land. There was no rain, but there was plenty of wind. The wind created so many dust storms, the area became known as the **Dust Bowl**. Millions of families were forced to relocate.

In **Russia** in **1921**, during a drought along the Volga river basin, five million people starved to death. **China** experienced a severe drought between **1876** and **1879**.

WILDFIRES

Eeek! That's fast!

Wildfires can start in the blink of an eye. They spread quickly through trees and other plants in a forested area. They can also jump to homes and other buildings.

A wildfire can spread through trees at a speed of about 6.7 miles per hour. A fire moves more than twice that fast when it is burning its way across grassy ground.

HOW DO WILDFIRES START?

More than half the wildfires that blaze around the globe are started by **people**, either accidentally or on purpose. The rest come about because of the **dry** conditions in an area with a lot of trees and other plants. In the United States and Canada, a bolt of **lightning** striking a tree starts most forest fires.

Forest fire

Firefighters tackle a forest fire

WHERE DO A LOT OF FOREST FIRES TAKE PLACE?

An area has to have enough **moisture** for part of the year to allow for trees and other plants to grow. But when a place goes through a long **dry period**, the greenery dries out. Australia, Southeast Asia, southern Europe, and parts of the United States and Canada have long, hot, dry summers. That makes **forest fires** fairly common seasonal events.

WHAT HAPPENS TO ANIMALS IN A FOREST FIRE?

Forestry experts say most animals manage to escape from forest fires. They know because they examine a **burned** forest after the fires have been put out and find very few animal remains. The **challenge** for animals that escape a fire is to find a new place to live.

ARCTIC

NORTH
AMERICA

PACIFIC

ATLANTIC

SOUTH
AMERICA

WHEN THE
EARTH
MOVES

Whether an earthquake shakes the ground with
enough force to break apart buildings, or thousands
of pounds of snow barrel down the slope of a
mountain, there's no mistaking the power of the
Earth when its elements shift and move.

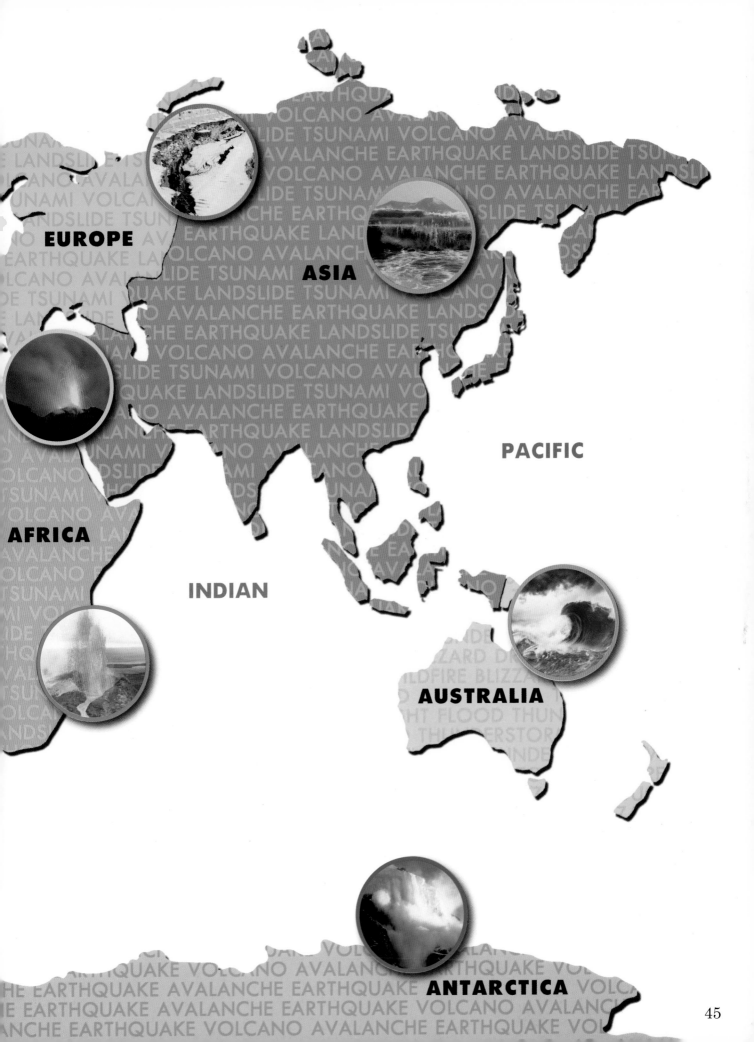

EUROPE

ASIA

PACIFIC

AFRICA

INDIAN

AUSTRALIA

ANTARCTICA

45

EARTHQUAKES

It comes without warning. Suddenly, the Earth shakes. Buildings crack, things tumble, and debris comes crashing down.

Hold on, Pluto! It's gonna get bumpy!

After an earthquake, a number of smaller tremors or aftershocks might continue for several days.

WHAT CAUSES AN EARTHQUAKE?

When two pieces of the Earth, called plates, knock into one another or shift suddenly, an **earthquake** can result. The plates usually move very slowly, at a rate of about 2 inches per year. Many earthquakes happen about 6 miles below the surface. The place where an earthquake starts in the ground is called the **hypocenter**. The place directly above the hypocenter on the surface is called the **epicenter**.

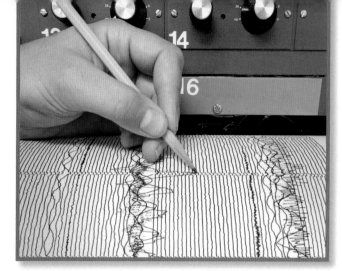
Seismograph

HOW IS AN EARTHQUAKE MEASURED?

The **magnitude**, or energy, released by an earthquake is measured by a mathematical formula called the **Richter scale**. The Richter scale relies on information scientists receive from **seismographs**. These record the vibrations of the Earth during an earthquake. Scientists consider a large earthquake to be one that registers **6.0** or higher on the Richter scale.

Damage from the 1985 earthquake in Mexico

HOW HIGH CAN THE RICHTER SCALE GO?

Scientists have not set a limit to the Richter scale. They doubt there could be an earthquake that reaches 10.0 or higher in magnitude—but they don't rule it out! In May 1960, southern **Chile** in South America experienced a **9.5** magnitude earthquake. It was the biggest one **recorded** in the 20th century. More than 1,500 people died, and two million were left homeless.

Building destroyed by an earthquake

47

EARTHQUAKES

Most earthquakes occur along cracks in the surface of the Earth called faults. A fault can be short or stretch for thousands of miles.

Gawrsh! For once, it's not my fault!

Most of the world's earthquakes happen in and around the Pacific Ocean. This area is called the circum-Pacific. It is also known as the "Ring of Fire," partly because there are also a lot of volcanoes there.

WHAT WERE SOME OF THE MOST DESTRUCTIVE EARTHQUAKES?

Damage from the 2010 earthquake in Haiti

In 1556 in **Shaanxi, China**, an **8.0** magnitude earthquake killed 830,000 people. Damage was reported as far as 500 miles away from the epicenter. In 1755 an earthquake of **8.7** in magnitude shook the city of **Lisbon, Portugal**. Crumbling buildings, floods, and fires killed one quarter of Lisbon's population. The Great Tokyo Earthquake shook the **Tokyo-Yokohama** area in Japan in 1923. The earthquake, at 7.9 in magnitude, led to severe firestorms and costly damage.

CAN EARTHQUAKES BE PREDICTED?

No. But scientists can figure out the **likelihood** of where an earthquake might happen and how major it might be. California in the U.S. has a lot of earthquakes. This is due to the **San Andreas Fault**, which runs through the state for about 800 miles.

San Andreas Fault

HOW DID ANCIENT CULTURES EXPLAIN EARTHQUAKES?

They created **myths** and **legends** to explain what caused an earthquake. In an **Indian** legend, eight elephants held up the Earth. When one got tired and lowered his head, an earthquake happened. **Japan** had the story of Namazu, a giant catfish who liked to play pranks. The gods kept Namazu under a rock. When he struggled to get free, he moved the rock and an earthquake happened.

49

TSUNAMIS

A tsunami happens when massive ocean waves smack the shore with deadly force. Sometimes there is a warning. But other times, the waves come in an instant, destroying everything in their path.

See ya real soon-ami!

A tsunami is a series of tall ocean waves called a wave train. It begins out at sea and travels at high speeds toward the shoreline.

WHAT CAUSES A TSUNAMI?

An **earthquake** that occurs underneath the ocean floor can cause one. This kind of earthquake is called a **submarine** earthquake. This kind can cause ocean water to slosh so much that a wave train forms.

An erupting **volcano**, a massive landslide, or a large amount of ice breaking off a glacier can also trigger a tsunami. So can a meteor falling from space!

Stormy waves

HOW HIGH
CAN A TSUNAMI WAVE BE?
HOW FAST
CAN IT TRAVEL?

A wave can be taller than **98 feet**— that's taller than a stack of 16 men standing on each other's shoulders!

Tsunamis have been clocked moving through ocean water at speeds of **500 miles per hour**!

HOW FAR
CAN A TSUNAMI TRAVEL?

Tsunamis happen most often along the **Pacific Rim**, on shorelines bordering the Pacific Ocean. The ocean floor there has lots of fault lines underneath, which make submarine earthquakes possible.

A **tsunami** can hit shore thousands of miles from where it begins. For example, a 9.5 magnitude earthquake shook Chile, South America, in 1960. The quake caused so much bouncing that a tsunami wave train formed. The train traveled **10,000 miles** to Honshu, Japan, where 10-foot-tall waves killed more than 150 people.

TSUNAMI EVACUATION ROUTE

VOLCANOES

Many ancient cultures told stories about angry gods causing volcanoes to erupt. But it's all part of the normal, natural—and sometimes deadly—workings of the Earth.

Aw, pickle juice! That's hot!

Each year between 50 and 70 volcanoes erupt. Many other volcanoes are dormant (still capable of erupting), but an extinct volcano no longer erupts.

WHAT EXACTLY IS A VOLCANO?

A **volcano** looks like a **mountain** because it *is* one. But it has a unique peak. A volcano has been formed by the buildup of its **eruptions** over time. The volcano is really the opening or vent through which eruptions happen. A mountain builds up around that vent.

Lava flow

Volcanic peak

Arenal Volcano erupting in Costa Rica

WHY DOES A VOLCANO ERUPT?

Molten (melted) rock lies deep inside the Earth, where it is constantly moving. Also called **magma**, the molten rock (which is lighter than solid rock) travels up through the layers of the Earth. When it **bursts** through the vent in a volcano, along with volcanic gases and ash, it is called an eruption.

ARE VOLCANOES FOUND ALL OVER THE WORLD?

Volcanoes can be found on all seven continents and several islands around the world. Even Antarctica has over a dozen volcanoes. This includes **Mount Erebus**, the world's southernmost active volcano. Mount Erebus has a lake made of lava! A **lava** lake forms when lava fills a crater in a volcano. This crater is 820 feet wide, nearly 330 feet deep, and full of molten lava!

Mount Erebus

53

VOLCANOES

Uh, now what?

The most dangerous part of a volcanic eruption isn't the lava. People are usually more in danger from the fast-moving mud slides or other debris triggered by an eruption.

When volcanoes are triggered by underwater earthquakes, the resulting tsunamis can kill more people than the eruption.

Mount Pelée in Martinique

WHAT ARE SOME HISTORIC ASH FLOWS?

One of the deadliest **ash flows** happened on the island of **Martinique**. In 1902, **Mount Pelée** erupted and destroyed the city of St. Pierre. The entire city was burned in minutes, killing more than 25,000 people.

Volcanic ash showered down over the ancient Italian city of Pompeii in 79 A.D. when **Mount Vesuvius** erupted. 2,000 people were killed and Pompeii was destroyed.

HAVE ANY LONG-DORMANT VOLCANOES ERUPTED RECENTLY?

One of the biggest volcanic eruptions of the 20th century was at **Mount Pinatubo** in the Philippines in 1991. The volcano had not erupted for **600 years**. When it blew, it sprayed millions of tons of ash over thousands of miles. In some places, the **ash** was hundreds of feet deep!

HOW ARE VOLCANIC ERUPTIONS MEASURED?

Scientists use the **Volcanic Explosivity Index** to rate the size and severity of an eruption from 0 to 8. Volcanoes that erupt daily, such as Stromboli in **Italy** and Mt. Kilauea on **Hawaii**, rate at 0 or 1 on the index. Volcanoes that erupt once in tens of thousands of years receive 8 as a rating.

Stromboli in Italy

Mount Pinatubo erupting

55

INSIDE THE **EARTH**

I'd move mountains for you, Minnie!

What do an **earthquake**, a **tsunami**, and a **volcano** have in common? They all begin on or below the surface of the Earth.

A LOOK AT **LAYERS**

The Earth is made up of **three layers**. The outer layer, the brittle and breakable **crust**, is the thinnest. The crust beneath the oceans is only about 3 miles thick. Under continents, it averages 18 miles thick, and under mountain ranges, about 62 miles. One layer down is the **mantle**, at 1,800 miles thick. It's made of extremely hot, semisolid rock. The deeper the mantle goes, the hotter it gets—from 900°F to 7,200°F! Rocks keep melting and moving, which causes earthquakes and volcanoes.

The **core**, the innermost layer, can reach 12,600°F! The core is made up of a solid inner part and a liquid outer part measuring about 4,200 miles across. Most of it is iron.

PASSING **PLATES**

Under Earth's crust where it meets the mantle are huge slabs of rock called **tectonic plates**. Some may be up to 90 miles thick! They sit on top of the hottest and least-solid part of the mantle, so they move. Most of the time, we don't feel the plates **shifting**. But when they move suddenly, bump each other, or pull apart, we feel it as an earthquake!

Oil refinery

ENERGY
FROM THE INSIDE OUT

Traditional **energy** sources come from inside the Earth: coal, oil, and natural gas. They are called **fossil fuels** because they come from the remains of ancient living things. These can't be replaced once they're removed from the Earth. But the Earth itself offers **geothermal** energy. Its heat can be turned into electricity! A well drilled into the Earth pumps hot steam out to a power plant. There it's used to generate electricity.

Metamorphic rocks

EARTHLY
MINERALS

There are around **3,700** known minerals found in the Earth's crust. Minerals such as **quartz**, graphite, and **gold** can be found in our pencils, medicines, glasses, thermometers, and in the roofing, wiring, and plumbing materials used in our homes.

EARTH ROCKS

The Earth's crust is made up of different kinds of rocks. There's **igneous** rock—volcanic lava and ash that has cooled—as well as **sedimentary** and **metamorphic** rock. Sedimentary rock is made up of broken-down bits of rocks. Metamorphic rock forms deep within the Earth when heat and pressure "cook" igneous or sedimentary rocks.

Coal miners in mine shaft

37

LANDSLIDES

Let's make mud pies!

In a landslide, rocks, mud, and other debris start out at the top of a steep incline and pick up speed and force as they come barreling down.

Some landslides occur due to rain or snowmelt, while others are triggered by an earthquake or a volcanic eruption.

Landslide in Brazil

WHERE WERE SOME LANDSLIDES TRIGGERED BY RAIN OR SNOWMELT?

Every year, massive **landslides** take place during rainy seasons. Both Brazil and **Uganda** experienced large landslides in 2010 due to intense rainfall. That was also a bad year for landslides in the northern part of India; heavy downpours triggered **mud slides**. Over the years, **Japan** has had several severe landslides triggered by rain. In Tibet, in 2000, 109 people died from a landslide triggered by rapid snowmelt.

Damage caused by a mud slide

WHERE WERE SOME LANDSLIDES TRIGGERED BY VOLCANOES?

In **Indonesia** in 1919, 104 villages were destroyed or damaged by **mud slides** triggered after the Kelut Volcano erupted. More than 5,000 died. In the United States, when **Mount Saint Helens** erupted in 1980, the heat from the lava caused the snow at the top of the mountain to melt. This triggered enormous landslides of rocks and other debris. Enough material came down the slope of the volcano to fill **250 million** dump trucks!

Earthquake damage on Montserrat Island

WHERE WERE SOME LANDSLIDES TRIGGERED BY EARTHQUAKES?

The **Haiyuan** earthquake in China's Gansu Province in **1920** was a big one. It measured **7.8** on the Richter scale. The resulting **landslides** caused more than 100,000 deaths. From Mexico and El Salvador in Central America to Alaska in North America to Peru in South America to **Pakistan** in Asia, landslides triggered by earthquakes have cost thousands of people their lives.

AVALANCHES

The force and weight of thousands of
pounds of snow racing down the slopes
of a mountain is a dangerous thing.
In an avalanche, a person can be
buried in an instant!

Buried by snow? Oh, no!

Every year, about one
million avalanches happen
on snow-covered slopes
around the world!

WHAT WERE SOME OF THE WORST AVALANCHES?

In **Peru** in 1970, a wall of snow 3,000 feet wide charged down Mount Huascaran at **130 miles per hour**. In four minutes it buried the ski resort of Yungay, killing more than 20,000 people.

Galtur, Austria, was a ski resort nestled at the foot of the Alps. In 1999, **300,000 tons** of snow tumbled down the mountain and crashed into the resort, killing 31 people.

Avalanche on an Antarctic glacier

WHAT CAUSES AN AVALANCHE?

Snow that covers mountains builds up over time in several layers. The **layers** can each be of a different quality: one can be very hard and icy, or very soft and loose, or somewhere in between. When two of the layers don't **bind together** properly and one of the layers gives way, look out!

HOW DO THEY FIND PEOPLE BURIED IN AN AVALANCHE?

One of the best and fastest ways to find someone buried under an avalanche is to send out a team of **rescue dogs**. The dogs are trained to **sniff** for people and can detect someone from about 40 feet away. Rescue dogs are much more effective than **probe poles**.

Rescuers use probe poles to **poke** into the snow, hoping to hit a person who is buried **underneath**. One study says that one dog can cover an area in one-eighth the time needed by 20 people searching with probe poles.

GLOSSARY

Anemometer—a device that measures wind speed

Avalanche—runaway snow tumbling down the slope of a mountain

Beaufort scale—a rating scale for wind force

Black smoker—an underwater volcano

Blizzard—the most severe type of a snowstorm, with winds blowing over 35 miles per hour for at least 3 hours

Core—the innermost part of the Earth; it has two layers, a liquid outer layer and a solid inner core.

Crust—the outermost layer of the Earth

Cyclone—a hurricane-like storm that forms over the Indian Ocean and rotates in a clockwise direction

Diameter—the width across a circle

Doppler radar—equipment used to monitor severe storms, such as tornadoes

Dormant (volcano)—a volcano still capable of erupting

Drought—a condition where an area has a severe shortage of water

Earthquake—a violent shaking of the Earth causing damage and devastation

El Niño—an unusual warming of sea-surface temperatures in the central part of the Pacific Ocean along and near the equator and along the coasts of Peru and Ecuador

Epicenter—the central point of an earthquake on the Earth's surface

Equator—an imaginary line that circles the center of the Earth

Eruption—when magma (molten rock), volcanic gases, and ash burst through the opening of a volcano

Evaporate—to change from liquid into a vapor

Extinct (volcano)—a volcano that no longer erupts

Eye (hurricane)—the central part of a hurricane where winds are relatively calm and there is little or no rain

Eyewall—layer of a hurricane closest to the center where wind is strongest

Famine—a severe shortage of food resulting in widespread hunger

Flood—a very large amount of water that overflows from a body of water and covers previously dry land

Fossil fuels—natural energy sources from inside the Earth (coal, gas, oil) that are the remains of long-dead creatures

Frostbite—damage caused to fingers, toes, or any part of the body exposed to extreme or prolonged cold

Geothermal energy—energy created by the Earth's natural heat or steam

Hurricane—a severe rainstorm with winds in excess of 74 miles per hour that forms over the Atlantic Ocean

Hydroelectricity—electricity generated by water

Hypocenter—the central point of an earthquake inside the Earth

Hypothermia—when body temperature drops four degrees and the body starts to shut down

Lava—melted rock that flows out of a volcano

Levee—a barrier built between a body of water and the surrounding land to prevent flooding

Magma—rocks inside the Earth that have melted from heat; also called molten rock

Magnitude—the unit used to measure the energy released by an earthquake

Mantle—the middle layer inside the Earth, where temperatures can reach 7,200°F

Meteorologist—someone who studies and predicts or forecasts the weather

Molten—changed into liquid form by heat; melted

Monsoon—a seasonal change in wind direction that brings heavy rainfall to an area

Plateau—an area of flat, high ground

Precipitation—water or moisture that falls from clouds, including rain, snow, and hailstones

Richter scale—a ratings system that measures the magnitude of an earthquake

Rogue waves—giant wave that rise up to 100 feet out of the sea; also called "killer" or "freak" waves

Satellite—an instrument launched into space that collects and transmits scientific information

Seismograph—an instrument that records vibrations or movements of the Earth

Storm surge—when ocean water rises due to a storm and crashes onto the land

Tectonic plates—a dozen or more large pieces of crust and mantle inside the Earth that shift and move and cause earthquakes

Tornado—a funnel-shaped cloud bringing rain, hail, and wind speeds in excess of 65 miles per hour

Tsunami—a series of tall ocean waves that travel at high speeds and crash onto the shore with deadly force

Typhoon—a hurricane-like storm with winds in excess of 74 miles per hour that forms over the western Pacific Ocean and moves into the China Sea

Upwelling—the process of deep ocean water rising toward the surface

Volcano—an opening or vent in the Earth's surface, usually on top of a mountain, through which lava, gas, and ash erupt

Wave train—the series of waves in a tsunami

INDEX

PHOTO CREDITS